Kisses·Kisses·Kisses

by Jenny Miglis

illustrated by Tammie Lyon

Kisses, kisses, there are so many kinds.
How many different kisses can you find?

There are loud smacking sound kisses.

And clowning around kisses.

Fluttering
butterfly kisses.

And Momma's here,
don't cry kisses.

No more frown kisses.

Upside-down kisses.

Ticklish kisses on the toes.

Eskimo kisses on the nose.

Just you and me kisses.

Salty sea kisses.

I love you to the moon kisses.

Kisses good-bye and kisses hello.

The kind of kisses grandpa blows.

Funny face kisses.

Out of place kisses.

There are big juicy, wet kisses,

And kisses soft and small.

But the kisses that YOU give
Are the very best of all.

There are grandpa's big bear hugs
And tiny teddy bear hugs, too.

And the best hugs of all . . .
Are the ones from me to you!

A kiss and a hug
and a wish good-night.

Hugs that are loose, and hugs that are tight.

And new glasses,
I can see hugs!

There are I skinned my knee hugs.

Granny's all around hugs.

Lost and then found hugs.

And down the slide at the park hugs.

There are afraid of the dark hugs.

And hugs that hug
away all your cares.

There are hugs you
find in rocking chairs.

My tooth is loose hugs.

I spilled my juice hugs.

And we didn't win hugs.

Learned to swim hugs.

And I see you hugs.

Hugs, Hugs, they're everywhere.
What's your favorite hug to share?

There are peek-a-boo hugs.

Hugs·Hugs·Hugs

by Jenny Miglis

illustrated by Tammie Lyon